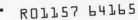

The Morning the Sun
Refused to Rise

Other Books Written and Illustrated
by Glen Rounds

OL' PAUL, THE MIGHTY LOGGER

THE BLIND COLT

STOLEN PONY

LONE MUSKRAT

WILD ORPHAN

THE TREELESS PLAINS

THE PRAIRIE SCHOONERS

WILD HORSES OF THE RED DESERT

ONCE WE HAD A HORSE

THE COWBOY TRADE

THE DAY THE CIRCUS CAME TO LONE TREE

THE BEAVER: HOW HE WORKS

MR. YOWDER AND THE GIANT BULL SNAKE

MR. YOWDER, THE PERIPATETIC SIGN PAINTER:
    THREE TALL TALES

BLIND OUTLAW

MR. YOWDER AND THE TRAIN ROBBERS

WILD APPALOOSA

MR. YOWDER AND THE WINDWAGON

The Morning the Sun Refused to Rise

an original Paul Bunyan tale by
GLEN ROUNDS

HOLIDAY HOUSE/NEW YORK

Library of Congress Cataloging in Publication Data

Rounds, Glen, 1906–
The morning the sun refused to rise.

Summary: When the sun doesn't rise one morning, the
King of Sweden contacts Paul Bunyan and asks him to find
the cause of the catastrophe.
1. Bunyan, Paul (Legendary character)—Juvenile
fiction. [1. Bunyan, Paul (Legendary character)—Fiction.
2. Tall tales] I. Title.
PZ7.R761Mf 1984 [E] 83-49033
ISBN 0-8234-0514-1

Although it happened many, many years ago, it still seems strange that so few people now remember the terrible night when the Great Blizzard blowing across the top of the world brought such bitter cold that the Earth froze tight to its axle and came to a complete stop. And even fewer have heard of the panic and suffering that spread across the world the next morning, when for the first time in history, the sun refused to rise.

And it is only in one or two crumbling copies of the oldest newspapers that one can find the account of how Paul Bunyan, the Giant Logger, found the cause of the catastrophe and by superhuman effort accomplished the seemingly impossible task of setting the world to turning again.

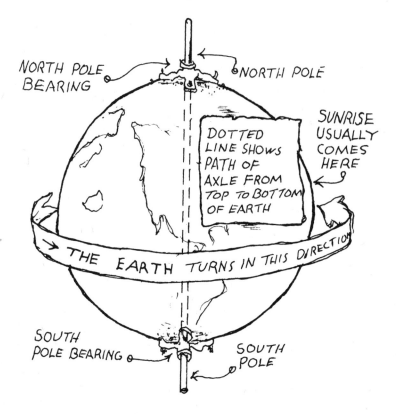

It is a well-known fact that the Earth spins on a great axle running through its center from top to bottom (see diagram). The top end turns in a huge bearing set in the ice, and sticks up several feet in the air. This end is called the North Pole. The other end sticks out of another bearing at the bottom of the world below South America (refer to diagram), and is called the South Pole.

This spinning is arranged so that sunrise comes early every morning, followed by roughly twelve hours of sunshine to warm the people and give them light to do their work, if they have jobs. Sunset comes at the end of the day, bringing night for sleeping and things like that.

This arrangement has been going on for as long as anyone can remember, and up to the time we speak of had worked right well. But on this particular morning, with the Earth frozen to its axle, sunrise couldn't come!

However, the spinning of the Earth is a thing that ordinary people seldom notice, so the first sign that something was wrong was the fact that the roosters didn't crow.

In those days very few people had alarm clocks, so they depended on the roosters crowing at first light to wake them. But on this terrible morning, without the light that comes before sunrise to wake them, roosters all over the world continued to sleep. And the people, hearing no crowing, slept on past their usual getting-up time.

The few people who had alarm clocks, however, were wakened at their usual time. As they built their fires, they looked out their windows and noticed that it was still dark. But figuring it was simply an unusually cloudy morning, they went on about cooking their breakfasts by lamplight.

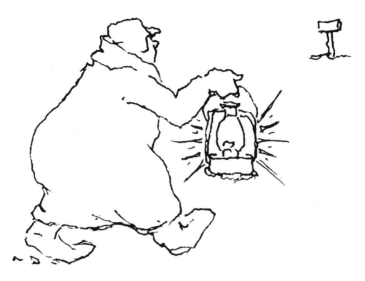

But when they'd eaten and were ready to go to work, the sky was still dark, even though their clocks said it was long past time for sunrise. So they began to worry. Putting on their coats and lighting their lanterns, they hurried to wake their sleeping neighbors with the news that sunrise was long overdue. Before long, crowds began to gather in the cold darkness, wondering what had happened. Looking up at the sky, they found the stars were shining—and realized that something more than a cloudy morning was holding sunrise back.

Something was terribly wrong. The cold was becoming steadily more bitter, and panic was spreading all over the world.

The desks of Kings, Presidents, Prime Ministers and even Senators were piled high with telegrams asking what had happened to sunrise.

But when the Government Experts looked in their books they found instructions for dealing with such things as revolutions, typhoons, hurricanes, forest fires, and hundreds of other kinds of disasters—but not a word about what to do when the sun refused to rise.

Apparently such a thing had never happened before. So then the governments called in their Scientists and Mathematicians to see if they could figure out what had happened. But even after these men had covered mountains of papers with figures, formulas, and the like they still hadn't discovered that the Earth had stopped turning and were as puzzled as everybody else.

The Mathematicians had just sent out for more paper and another box of pencils when the President got a telegram from the Eskimo whose job was to grease the North Pole bearing every morning. The telegram read: EARTH'S AXLE FROZEN IN BEARING STOP EARTH NOT TURNING STOP SIGNED MUCKLUK.

So at last the governments knew why sunrise hadn't come, and the Experts hurried to the North Pole. They tried to thaw the bearing out with blowtorches, but the cold was so great that the flames froze and dropped off as fast as they were lighted. And of course in that country there is no wood for fires.

Crowds of Government Experts bustled about, getting in each other's way, trying this and that while the Eskimos from the neighborhood looked on. But still the bearing remained frozen.

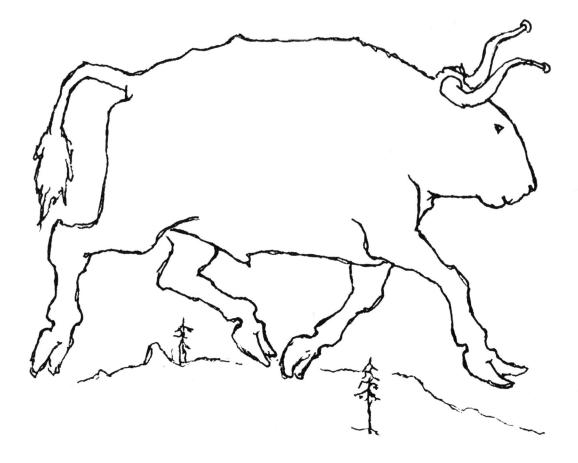

It is hard to know what might have happened if the King of Sweden hadn't thought of Paul Bunyan, the Mighty Logger, and Babe, his Great Blue Ox and constant companion.

Ol' Paul was the legendary giant who had invented logging and was known far and wide for his ability to do the impossible—and to often do it the hard way just for the fun of it.

It was common knowledge that with the help of

the Blue Ox and a crew of the most expert loggers in the world, there was nothing Ol' Paul couldn't fix, yank straight, tear down or rebuild.

Just how big Babe really was has long been a mat-
ter of debate among the Professors who write books

about such matters. But old newspaper accounts say that on a certain Sunday a crew of lumberjacks, having nothing better to do, set out to measure the Mighty Blue Ox.

By late afternoon they had managed to measure the distance between the Great Beast's eyes—seven-hundred-and-fifty-four ax handles, two-hundred-and-four cans of tomatoes (no. 10's), and a plug of Star chewing tobacco laid edgewise.

By the time they'd done that, the cooks were beating on the mess hall triangle, calling the men to supper, so they never did get around to measuring the rest of him. But it is a known fact that at every step Babe's hooves sank seven feet into the solid rock—and the many small lakes in the North Country are said to be his old tracks, now filled with water.

The King of Sweden remembered Ol' Paul from the time he'd made what was then the greatest log drive ever—floating three-and-a-half million logs from the North Woods to Sweden. And they'd been friends ever since, so now the King had his hired man hitch a team to the Royal Sleigh—the oceans were frozen to the bottom at the time or he'd have taken his rowboat—and drove over to Ol' Paul's camp.

Ol' Paul was glad to see the King again, after all those years. He shook hands with him and got out a box of cigars, then sent a flunky over to the mess hall for a pot of fresh coffee. After they'd sat a while in Ol' Paul's office, smoking cigars and drinking coffee, the King asked Ol' Paul if he'd heard about sunrise not having come that morning.

Ol' Paul's camp at the time was so far back in the North Woods that it was always bitterly cold there—and the trees were so thick that it was almost always as dark as night, even in the daytime. So neither Ol' Paul nor any of his men had noticed that sunrise was missing that day. He was quite surprised by the news.

But before he'd really gotten started thinking about the problem, there was a banging on the door and a delegation of Government Men came in with a letter from the President asking Ol' Paul to try and do something to get the Earth turning so sunrise could come again.

Paul listened to them, told them to tell the President that he'd see what he could do, then sent them to the mess hall for a bite to eat before they started back. The King had brought his own lunch so Ol' Paul walked him to his Royal Sleigh, shook hands with him again and gave him a handful of his special cigars before he drove off. Then Ol' Paul put on his heaviest fur coat (it was said to have been made from four-hundred-and-nine prime bearskins trimmed with sealskin at the collar), and walked over to the North Pole to see what had to be done.

The Great Blizzard was still blowing, and Ol' Paul found that the Government Men had all gone back to Washington or someplace to get warm. The only people in sight were a few Eskimos who lived in the neighborhood.

While the Eskimos watched, Ol' Paul took hold of the axle, but even his great strength couldn't move it. It was not only frozen into the bearing but he was certain from the feel of it that the axle was frozen tight in its shaft all the way down to the South Pole at the bottom of the Earth. Before he set about getting the world to turning again, he'd have to think of a way to thaw the ice out of the frozen bearing and the axle shaft.

Taking off a mitten to scrape frost from his beard, Ol' Paul leaned against the North Pole, thinking at top speed. He thought for a while, looking south, without thinking of anything that would work. So for a change he moved around to the other side of the Pole to think some more and found that he was again looking south. It hadn't occurred to him before that from the North Pole all directions are south. He was still thinking furiously when he happened to notice a surprising number of dead polar bears scattered about on the snow.

These bears have very warm fur and seldom mind the cold, even swimming around among pieces of floating ice as they hunt seals and other game. But now the cold was so great that even they were beginning to freeze to death. From where he stood Ol' Paul could see dozens of them, already frozen stiff, lying around on the snow.

Walking over to the nearest one, he ran his hands through the thick fur. And underneath the fur he felt the thick layer of fat that in ordinary times helped keep the bear safe from the cold.

And that was when Ol' Paul saw the solution to the problem of getting the frozen bearings thawed out. Polar bear skins and polar bear oil! That was the answer.

It took him only a few minutes to work out the details in his mind. Then he wrote a note to his woods boss, Shot Gunderson, asking him to hitch Babe to the big work sled and bring a crew of men, some long timbers, his special toolbox and all the big pea-soup kettles from the mess hall to the North Pole. Calling the fastest runner among the Eskimos, he handed him the note and the list and gave him a quarter to take them back to his camp in the North Woods.

Paul was all business now, and as soon as the messenger was on his way, he divided the rest of the Eskimos into two crews, promising them good pay for the job he had in mind.

One crew had dog teams and he put them to work loading dead polar bears onto the sleds, one at a time, and hauling them up close to the North Pole. And as fast as the bear carcasses were unloaded, the other crew started skinning them. The thick, warm pelts were put in one pile nearby, and the great layers of fat in another.

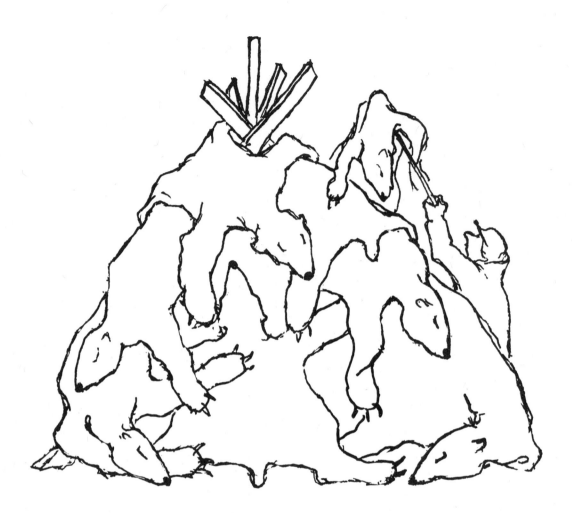

By the time the piles of bearskins and bear fat were as high as an Eskimo's head, Shot Gunderson came in sight driving Babe the Great Blue Ox hitched to the big sled loaded with the men and tools Ol' Paul had asked for.

Ol' Paul right away set the woods crew to building a sort of teepee frame of timbers over the end of the

North Pole—and then he had them cover it with several layers of polar bear skins, making a snug warm place to protect the men from the bitter wind.

As soon as the bearskin teepee was finished he had the biggest of the great kettles from the sled dragged and rolled inside—and set up right beside the frozen axle bearing.

Of course there was no wood in that part of the country, but several of Ol' Paul's men had worked at one time or another on whaling ships in the old days, and knew about using whale fat for fuel. Polar bear fat burns as well as whale fat and in a short time they had brisk fires burning and the kettles slowly filling with melted polar bear oil.

Then Ol' Paul had one man start pouring the hot oil, a dipper full at a time, onto the frozen bearing. Instead of congealing in the cold as the Government Men's axle grease had done, the polar bear oil soon soaked the frost out of the bearing, then started working its way down inside the frozen shaft. While the crew continued trying out more bear fat, Ol' Paul hired an Eskimo to take three of his most trustworthy men by dogsled down to the South Pole at the bottom of the world to watch for the bear oil to start dripping out of the axle bearing there.

But only one part of Ol' Paul's problems had been solved. For when the great axle was unfrozen from the bearings he still had to figure a way to start the world to spinning again—and he knew that would take some very hard thinking. Even a loaded wagon or sled is hard to get moving once it has stopped, and the Earth was many, many times heavier than the heaviest wagon. So while the men continued pouring hot polar bear oil down the axle shaft, Ol' Paul hurried back to camp to do some more thinking.

But when he got to his office he found his desk piled high with letters and telegrams from Kings and Presidents and the like, all wanting to know when he'd have the Earth turning so that sunrise could come again.

Ol' Paul had no doubts about being able to do the job, but reading and answering all those letters and telegrams would take up time he badly needed for thinking. So he had Johnny Inkslinger, his head bookkeeper, pick out a hundred-and-eighty men who could read and write, and turned the job over to them.

Then he went over to the mess hall to drink coffee while he did some real serious thinking. He sat there until ten o'clock, just drinking coffee and thinking, but still couldn't think of a way to get a thing as big as the world turning on its axle again. Finally it was ten or fifteen minutes after ten, and he didn't see how it could be done.

Ol' Paul had just refilled his fifteen-gallon coffee mug for the tenth time and was reaching for the can of condensed milk when he accidentally tipped over a jug of sourdough starter sitting on the back of the big range. Still stirring his coffee and thinking, he was watching the jug and listening to the odd gurgling sounds coming from inside it when, without warning, the cork blew out of the neck with a report like a rifle shot.

For a moment the jug lay there, spewing a stream of sourdough as powerful as the jet from a firehose nozzle. Then it took off like a skyrocket, straight across the mess hall! Tearing a great hole in the wall, the jug whizzed over the heads of the crowd of men outside, ploughed a deep furrow across the top of the mountain west of camp, and disappeared.

Ol' Paul stood there a minute or two, speechless with surprise. Then he let out a roar that blew out half of the mess hall windows.

"Rocket power!" he hollered. "Rocket power's the answer!"

Most rockets, even today, use gunpowder or some other explosive fuel for their power, but Ol' Paul saw no reason sourdough, which is known to be as powerful as any gunpowder ever made, shouldn't do as well. And he'd already figured out how he was going to use it.

To understand Ol' Paul's plan, one has to remember that in those days the map of the United States was much different from what it is now. Instead of the Appalachian and Rocky Mountain ranges being separated by the Middle West (as they are now), they were both in the western part of the country. The Rockies ran about where they are now, from Alaska into Mexico, while just a few miles to the east of them, across a wide valley, were the Appalachians. And all the land from there to the East Coast was still flat prairie.

Ol' Paul's plan was to use sourdough rocket power to push eastward against the Appalachians to start the world turning on its axle again. And in less than half an

ROCKY
MOUNTAINS

APPALACHIAN
MOUNTAINS

ATLANTIC
OCEAN

PLAINS

CALIFORNIA

PACIFIC
OCEAN

hour he had Babe hitched to his biggest sled, loaded with rock-drilling equipment and every crew he could spare.

Driving south between the two mountain ranges he unloaded a crew every half mile from Canada to Mexico and left them drilling tunnels into the side of the high mountain wall on the east side of the valley. By noon the men were all at work.

The entrances to these tunnels were small, so small that the men had to crawl on hands and knees as they worked. But further back the tunnels widened to form great cave-like chambers to hold the sourdough when it was ready (see diagram).

While the tunnels were being drilled, Ol' Paul went back to camp and put all the cooks, bull cooks, and flunkies to work hauling flour away and other such stuff to the Sourdough Lake on top of the mountain behind the mess hall. The little steamboat that usually ran only at night mixing sourdough for each morning's breakfast flapjacks now worked night and day. As soon as one batch was mixed and pumped into the great tank wagons, another was started. As each tank wagon was filled it was covered with more of the polar bear skins to keep the bubbling sourdough warm, and hitched onto the wagon ahead.

Just as the men were filling the last tank, an Indian brought Paul a message that bear oil was beginning to drip out around the South Pole bearing down on the bottom of the world. Paul made a quick trip up to the North Pole, took a firm grip on the axle and shook it. And sure enough, the bear oil had done the trick and the world's axle was free at last. Now all Ol' Paul had to do was get the Earth turning again and sunrise could come as it always had.

It was almost noon when Ol' Paul got back to camp, but word had just come that the last of the tunnels would be finished in a few minutes. So, hitching Babe to the head of the miles-long train of tank wagons, he drove at top speed to the valley between the two mountain ranges.

Without slowing down he had the men unhook a tank wagon by the mouth of each tunnel as he passed. One man was a little slow getting out of the way after he'd pulled the hitch pin, and broke his leg when he was run over. But otherwise the job went off without a hitch.

Ol' Paul's voice could be heard for almost any distance so now he gave the signal and all up and down the line men started pumping the warm, bubbling sourdough into the tunnels. As each tunnel was filled, the entrance was tightly plugged with a great stopper cut from one of the biggest redwood trees in California.

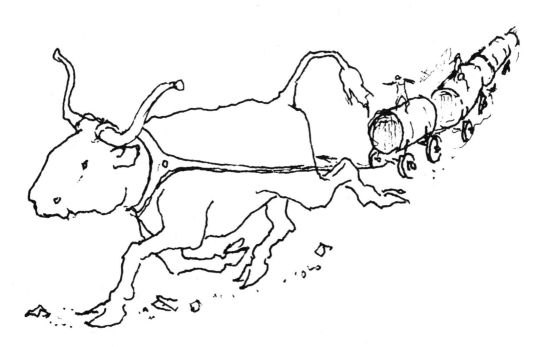

Of course it was still pitch dark, but nonetheless Ol' Paul and his men stood peering in the direction of the mountain ranges. At first nothing at all happened, and after a while the men began to shuffle their feet and wonder if all their work had been wasted—but Ol' Paul seemed confident as usual.

While they waited the King of Sweden drove up in his Royal Sleigh, saying he'd heard that Ol' Paul was using sourdough power to start the Earth turning again, and he wanted to watch. Ol' Paul shook hands with him and gave him a cigar, saying that the stuff should begin to work any minute now.

As soon as the last tunnel had been filled and the redwood plug driven tightly into place, Ol' Paul sent all the men and wagons back to his camp to be out of the way of what he knew was going to happen. Then he sent Eskimos across the country, warning folk to get their livestock undercover, and to stay near their cyclone cellars if they had them. After that there was nothing to do but wait and see if his plan was going to work.

And just then they felt a trembling in the Earth under their feet, very faint at first but enough to make the soles of their feet tingle. A little later they felt another trembling as well as small rumblings and creakings coming from deep in the ground. The King of Sweden was so excited that he used three matches to get his cigar lit. He'd finally got it going good when the redwood plug blew out of the first tunnel mouth with a terrible bang, louder than a hundred thunderclaps.

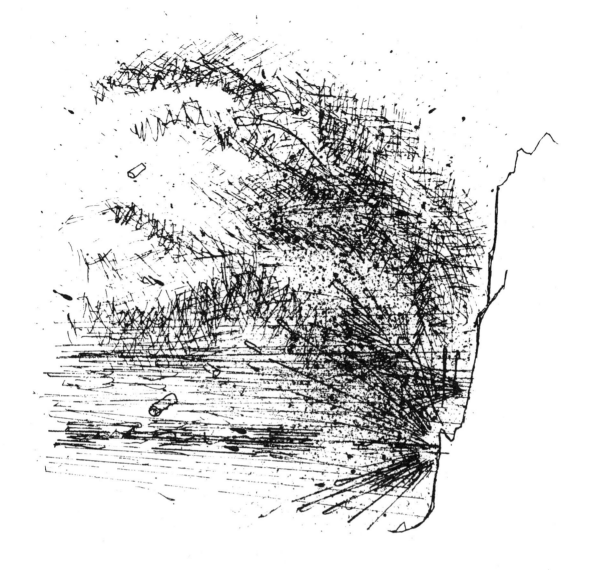

And one by one, a dozen at a time, the plugs began blowing out of the others. Never had the world heard such a banging, rumbling, whizzing and roaring as the great jets of steamy sourdough and sourdough gas roared out of the line of tunnel mouths, to strike the wall of the Rocky Mountains behind them.

The whole valley seemed to boil as the clouds of sourdough, sourdough gas, and dust rose high into the already dark sky! And the sounds of the roaring sourdough jets were almost drowned by the terrible cracking of splitting rock deep beneath the mountains. It is probable that such a sound had never before been heard since the world began. Frightened birds left their nests and flew blindly about, banging into mountain sides, trees and buildings.

Herds of large animals stampeded, tearing down fences and trampling fields of grain while smaller ones left their dens and swarmed in all directions. It was a time of wild confusion.

The ground underfoot continued to tremble, shake, and rock—but for a while longer nothing else happened—for the foundations of the mountains went deep into the center of the Earth.

Then suddenly, as Paul sighted a dark mountaintop against a low star, he saw that the Earth was moving! It stopped, then moved again. Slowly at first, then faster and faster the Earth began to turn.

Holding their hands over their ears, the watching men found that the shaking of the Earth made it difficult for them to keep on their feet. Even so, some shouted "Hooray!" and things like that, but nobody heard them.

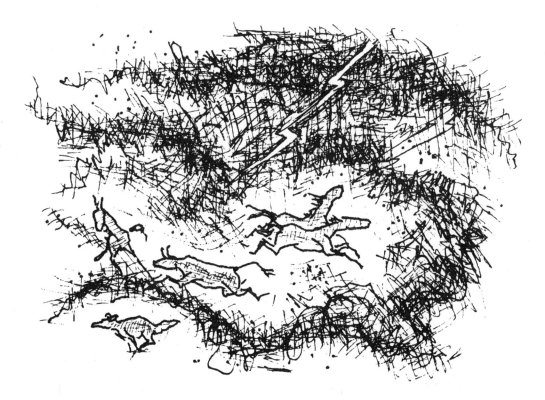

The roar of the sourdough jets and the fearful sounds of splitting rock went on until it seemed the whole Earth would come apart.

Then, the sky in the East began to lighten. All over the world people waved their hats and clapped each other on the back, while roosters everywhere took their heads from under their wings and started crowing for dawn.

The light in the East grew stronger and at 4:45 P.M. by the Government Men's watches, the first edge of the sun appeared over the horizon—and sunrise had come again!

All over the world people stood in the streets or on their doorsteps, cheering and clapping each other on the back. Once more Paul Bunyan had proved that he could do the impossible! And his picture was on the front page of all the papers.

But even so, not everybody was happy with the fantastic job Ol' Paul had done. For one thing, sunrise now came at 4:45 P.M., and this caused some complaint since folks were not used to the idea of getting up and going to work in the afternoon instead of the morning. But someone, remembering the way the government set clocks back or ahead for daylight saving time, suggested that everybody simply turn their clocks back ten hours and forty-five minutes—and that solved the problem.

But the most complaints came from the people living in the Appalachian Mountains. When daylight came that day they found that the power of Ol' Paul's sourdough rockets had pushed the entire Appalachian range fifteen-hundred miles to the East—where it stands to this day. So instead of living in Montana, Wyoming, Colorado, or some other western state, they were now citizens of West Virginia, Kentucky and Tennessee, and even North Carolina. They began to raise a clamor and talk of lawsuits because having been raised in the West they now had trouble understanding their new neighbors, who all talked Southern.

THE ROCKY MOUNTAINS STILL STAND IN THE WEST

NEW MIDWEST

BUT THE APPALACHIANS ARE NOW CLOSER TO THE ATLANTIC OCEAN

OL' PAUL'S SOURDOUGH POWER PUSHED THE APPALACHIAN RANGE NEARLY 2,000 MILES TO THE EAST, WHERE IT CAN BE SEEN TO THIS DAY!

But it all settled down after a while—some stayed and learned the language while others moved and looked for farms in the newly formed stretch of land between the Appalachians and the Rockies. That part of the country is now called the MIDWEST, and is right popular with a certain class of people.

Of course all the maps of the country east of the Rockies had to be redrawn, and building roads across the new MIDWEST was something of a problem and a burden to the taxpayers. But all in all, in the end, Ol' Paul's sourdough rockets did more good than harm.